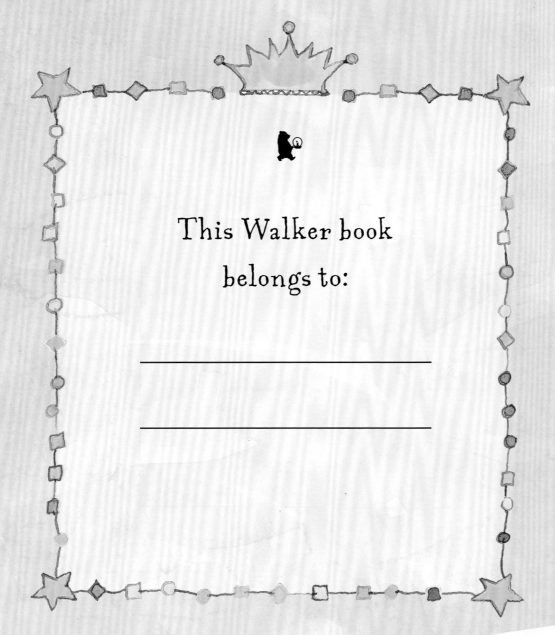

This Walker book

belongs to:

_____

_____

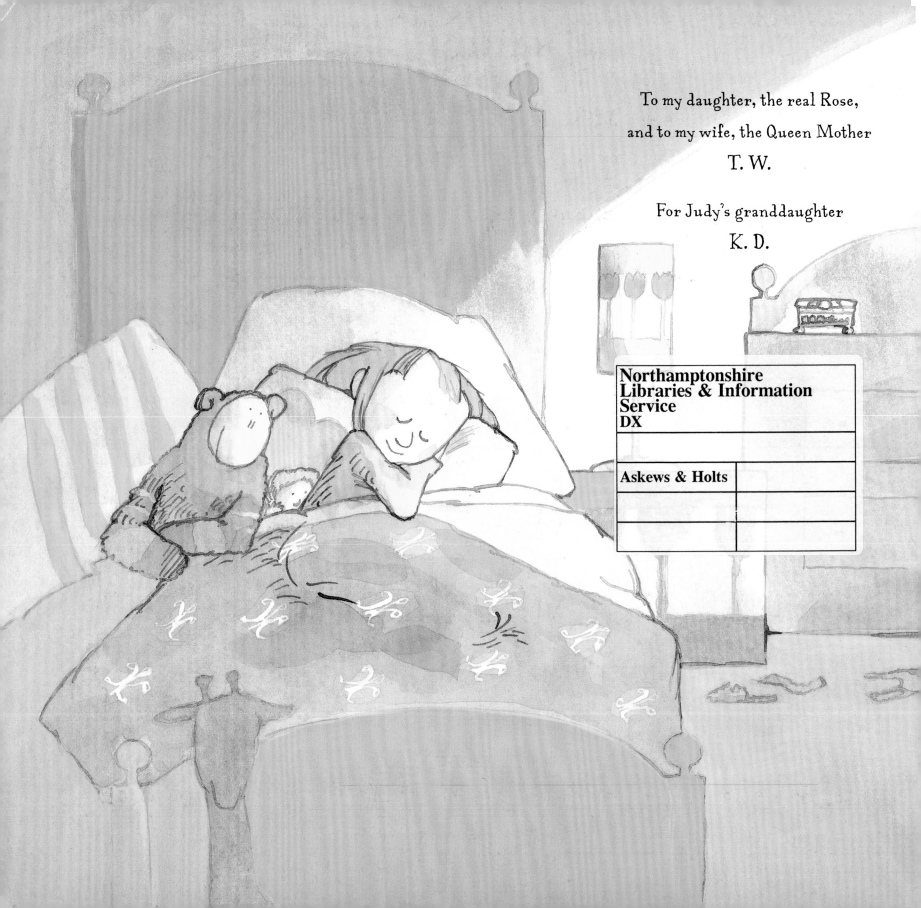

To my daughter, the real Rose,
and to my wife, the Queen Mother
T. W.

For Judy's granddaughter
K. D.

THE QUEEN OF FRANCE

Tim Wadham

illustrated by
Kady MacDonald Denton

WALKER BOOKS
AND SUBSIDIARIES
LONDON • BOSTON • SYDNEY • AUCKLAND

When Rose woke up that morning, she felt royal.

She opened the box of jewellery.

She put on the necklaces.

She put on the bracelets.

She went to the dressing-up basket.

She put on the crown.

The Queen of France went
to find Rose's mother.

"Hello, I am the Queen of France. Have you seen Rose?"

"No," said Rose's mother.

"I wonder where she could be," said the Queen of France.

"I hope she remembers to tidy her room," said Rose's mother.

"Why are you planting those bumpy sticks?" asked the queen.

"This is a rose bush, Your Majesty," said Rose's mother.

"It is ugly," said the queen.

"Yes, it is," said Rose's mother. "But it will soon grow green and beautiful, and lovely pink flowers will bloom on the stems. I named Rose after this flower."

"I see," said the queen. "May I touch it?"

"Yes, certainly," said Rose's mother. "But please be careful."

"Ouch!" said the queen. "I have pricked my royal finger."

"May I kiss it for you?" said Rose's mother.

"No," said the queen, "I have a Royal Physician for things like that. Goodbye."

"Goodbye," said Rose's mother.

The Queen of France went to find the Royal Physician.

"Hello!" she yelled. "I am the Queen of France."

Rose's father stopped the lawn mower.

"Are you by chance the Royal Physician?"

"No, I am Rose's father."

"Oh," said the queen. "My finger requires medical attention."

"I'm sorry," said Rose's father. "I hope you find the Royal Physician."

"So do I," said the queen. "By the way, have you seen Rose?"

"No," said Rose's father, "I thought she was in the garden. When you see her, please tell her that we are reading an exciting pirate story tonight."

"I won't forget," said the queen.

The Queen of France went to Rose's room.

She took off the necklaces.

She took off the bracelets.

She put them in the jewellery box.

She took off the crown.

She put it in the dressing-up basket.

She went to the hall cupboard.

She found a bandage and put it on her finger.

Then she put on a second one, just in case.

Then Rose went to find her mother.

"Mother, have you seen the Queen of France?" Rose asked.

"Why, yes," said Rose's mother, "she just left. She hurt her finger and went to look for the Royal Physician."

"Interesting," said Rose. "If you see the queen, please tell her that I am looking for her too."

Rose went to find the Queen of France.

She looked in her bedroom. The Queen of France was not there.

And her room was not tidy. She sighed. There were dirty clothes on the floor. Rose gathered them up and put them in the clothes basket. Her bed was all messy. She pulled up the covers and put her stuffed monkey on the pillow.

Rose went to the jewellery box.

She put on the necklaces.

She put on the bracelets.

She went to the dressing-up basket.

She put on the crown.

The Queen of France went to find Rose's mother.

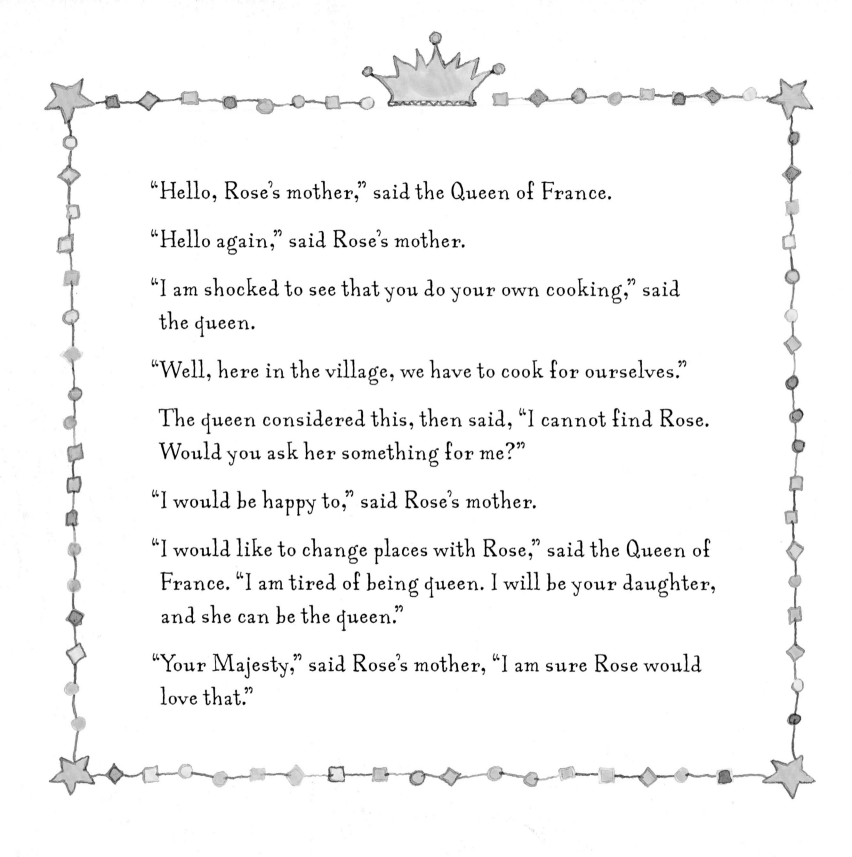

"Hello, Rose's mother," said the Queen of France.

"Hello again," said Rose's mother.

"I am shocked to see that you do your own cooking," said the queen.

"Well, here in the village, we have to cook for ourselves."

The queen considered this, then said, "I cannot find Rose. Would you ask her something for me?"

"I would be happy to," said Rose's mother.

"I would like to change places with Rose," said the Queen of France. "I am tired of being queen. I will be your daughter, and she can be the queen."

"Your Majesty," said Rose's mother, "I am sure Rose would love that."

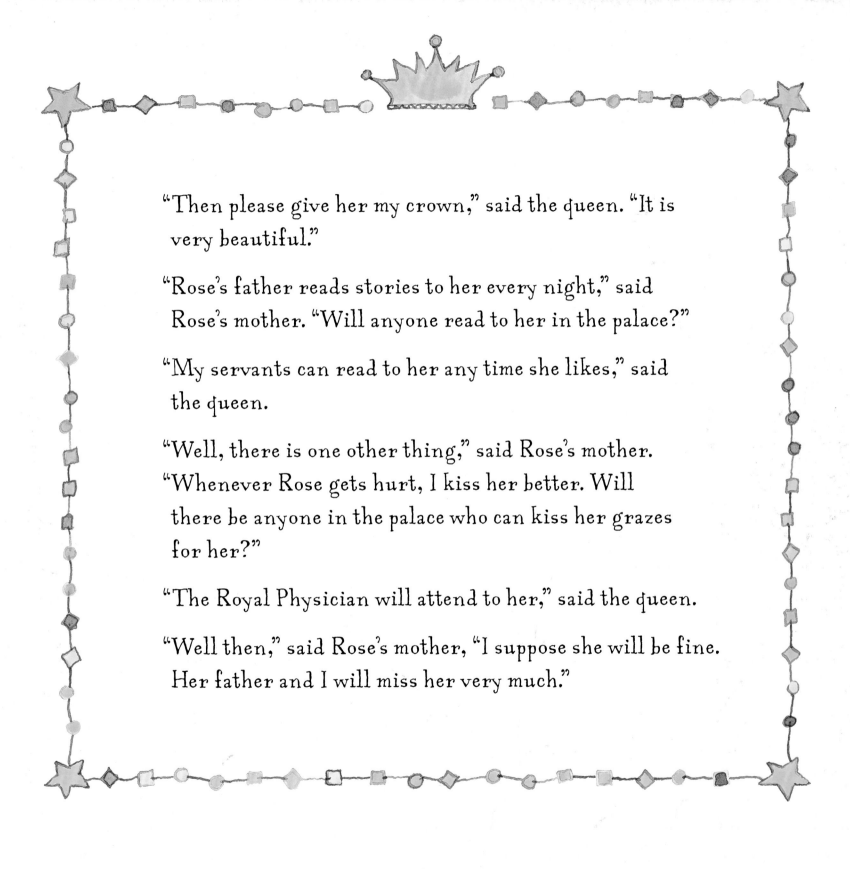

"Then please give her my crown," said the queen. "It is very beautiful."

"Rose's father reads stories to her every night," said Rose's mother. "Will anyone read to her in the palace?"

"My servants can read to her any time she likes," said the queen.

"Well, there is one other thing," said Rose's mother. "Whenever Rose gets hurt, I kiss her better. Will there be anyone in the palace who can kiss her grazes for her?"

"The Royal Physician will attend to her," said the queen.

"Well then," said Rose's mother, "I suppose she will be fine. Her father and I will miss her very much."

The queen thought about this. "Just how much will you miss her?" she asked.

"I will miss her infinity times infinity," said Rose's mother.

"That is a very large amount," said the queen. "If you would miss her that much, I'm afraid we cannot change places. Rose would have liked being queen, though. You never have to tidy your room. Well, goodbye."

"Goodbye," said Rose's mother. "If you see Rose, tell her that supper is ready."

The Queen of France turned and walked away.

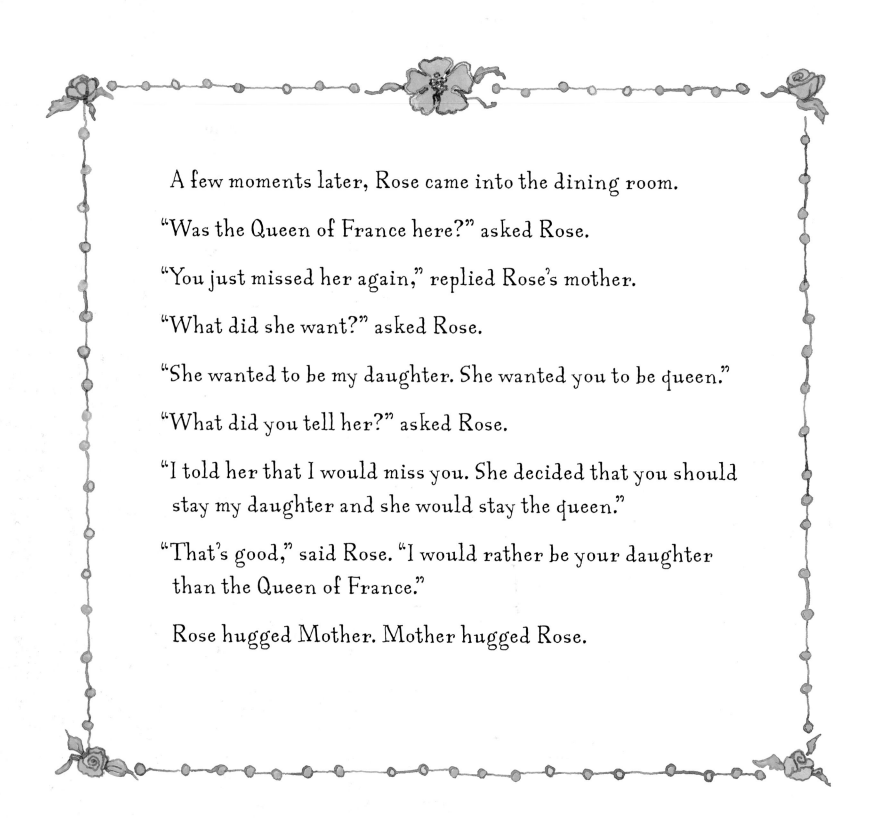

A few moments later, Rose came into the dining room.

"Was the Queen of France here?" asked Rose.

"You just missed her again," replied Rose's mother.

"What did she want?" asked Rose.

"She wanted to be my daughter. She wanted you to be queen."

"What did you tell her?" asked Rose.

"I told her that I would miss you. She decided that you should stay my daughter and she would stay the queen."

"That's good," said Rose. "I would rather be your daughter than the Queen of France."

Rose hugged Mother. Mother hugged Rose.

When Rose finished supper that evening, she felt ... scary.

"Perfect," said Rose.

Tim Wadham is a librarian who has served on many prestigious awards
committees and is very involved in children's theatre.
This is his first picture book. He lives in the USA, in Missouri.

Kady MacDonald Denton is an author and illustrator of books for children,
including the award-winning *A Visitor for Bear*, *A Bedtime for Bear* and
The Sniffles for Bear. She lives in Ontario, Canada.

ISBN 978-1-4063-2342-9   ISBN 978-1-4063-3205-6   ISBN 978-1-4063-3653-5

Available from all good booksellers

www.walker.co.uk

First published 2011 by Walker Books Ltd, 87 Vauxhall Walk, London SE11 5HJ ✦ This edition published 2012 ✦ 2 4 6 8 10 9 7 5 3 1 ✦ Text © 2011 Tim Wadham ✦
Illustrations © 2011 Kady MacDonald Denton ✦ The right of Tim Wadham and Kady MacDonald Denton to be identified as author and illustrator respectively of this
work has been asserted by them in accordance with the Copyright, Designs and Patents Act 1988 ✦ This book has been typeset in Aunt Mildred ✦ Printed in China ✦
All rights reserved ✦ No part of this book may be reproduced, transmitted or stored in an information retrieval system in any form or by any means, graphic, electronic
or mechanical, including photocopying, taping and recording, without prior written permission from the publisher ✦ British Library Cataloguing in Publication Data:
a catalogue record for this book is available from the British Library ✦ ISBN 978-1-4063-3997-0 ✦ www.walker.co.uk